The Day the Dog Dressed Like Dad

To our dads, Rudy and Jim

Published by Bloomsbury, New York and London
Distributed to the trade by Holtzbrinck Publishers

Library of Congress Cataloging-in-Publication Data
Amico, Tom.
The day the dog dressed like Dad / Tom Amico and James Proimos ; [pictures by James Proimos].
p. cm.
Summary: One day when Dad is out of town, the family dog decides to take over his role
by demanding some grub, taking the family on a picnic, and hogging the remote.
ISBN 1-58234-877-4 (alk. paper)
[1. Dogs—Fiction. 2. Family life—Fiction. 3. Humorous stories.] I. Proimos, James, ill. II. Title.
PZ7.A5163Day 2004   [E]—dc22
2003065345

First U.S. Edition 2004
Printed in Hong Kong/China
3 5 7 9 10 8 6 4 2

Bloomsbury USA Children's Books
175 Fifth Avenue
New York, NY 10010

All papers used by Bloomsbury Publishing are natural, recyclable products
made from wood grown in well-managed forests. The manufacturing processes
conform to the environmental regulations of the country of origin.

The Day the Dog Dressed Like Dad

by **Tom Amico** & **James Proimos**
Pictures by **James Proimos**

BLOOMSBURY
CHILDREN'S
BOOKS

One day my dad had
to go out of town.
I was just about
to tell my sister that
I was taking over
when the dog
came downstairs
dressed exactly like Dad.

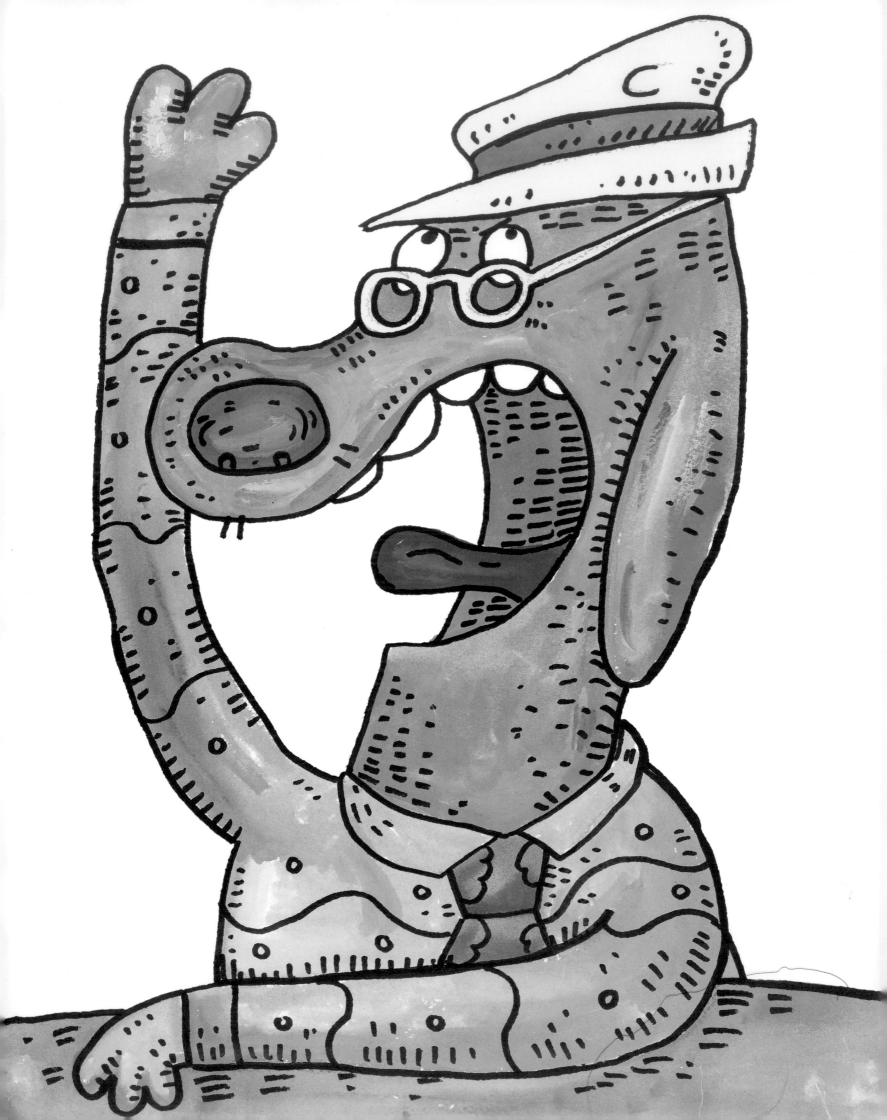

Like Dad,
he woke up
grouchy and
demanded
some grub.

Mom gave it to him.

He took us
on a picnic,
just like
Dad would.

He ate corn
on the cob
exactly
like Dad.

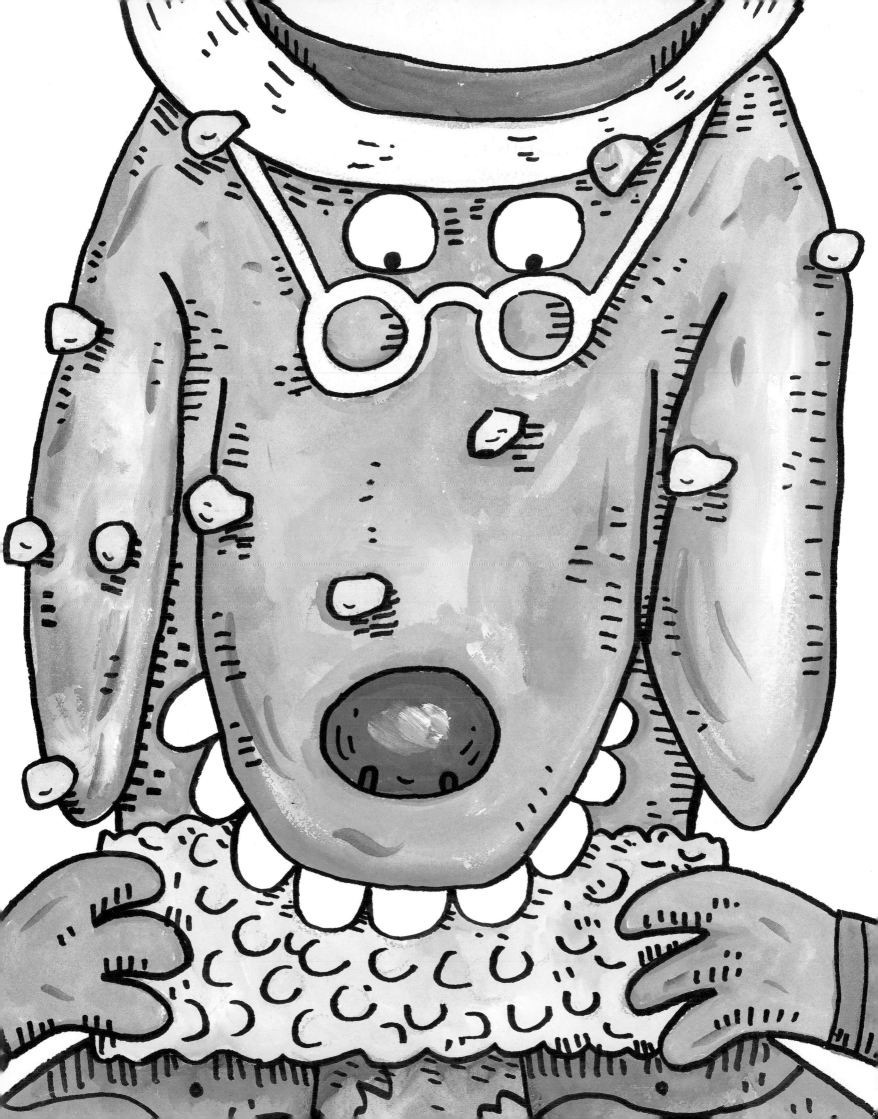

He saw a cat.
Unlike Dad,
he chased it.
But only
for a few
minutes.

On the way
back home
our dog barked
out orders,
like Dad.

I said, "Don't worry,
his bark is worse
than his bite."
My sister laughed
and laughed
and laughed.

For dinner
our dog
barbecued,
like Dad.

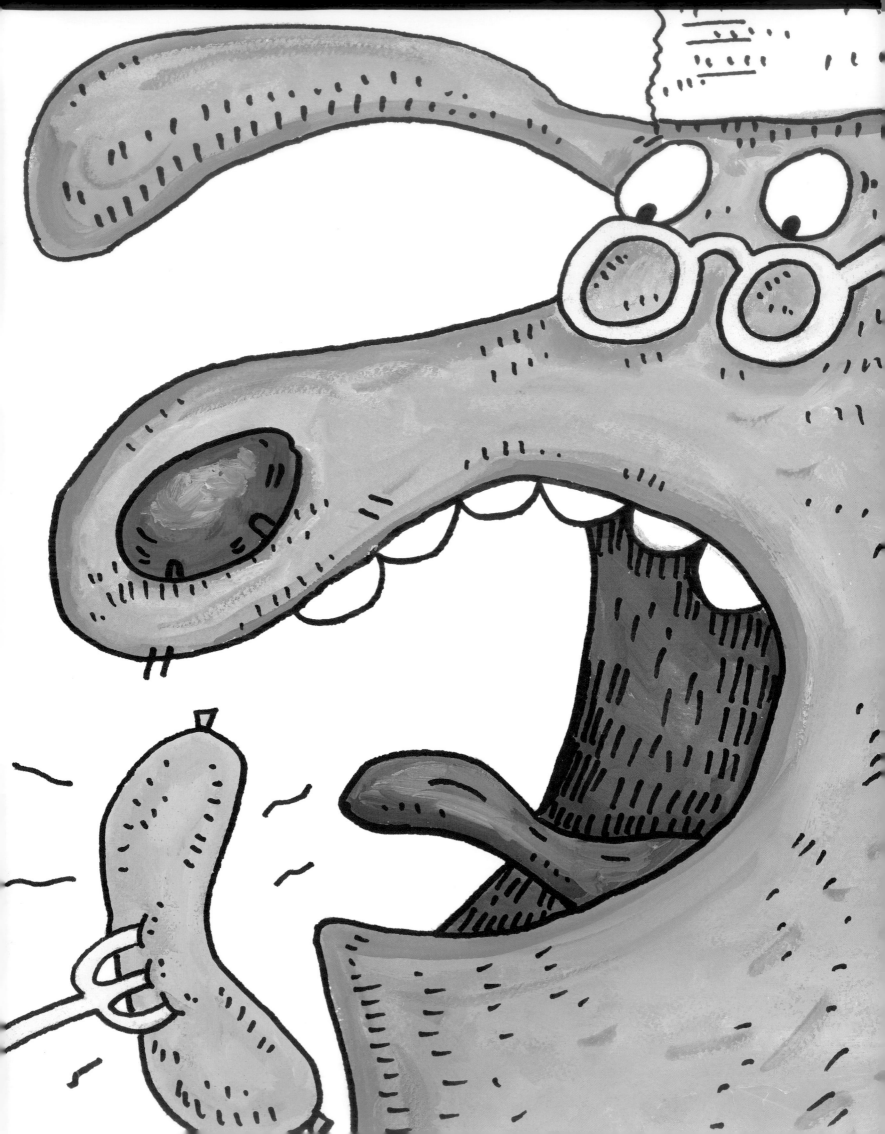

Except he
refused to make
hot dogs.

At the end
of the day,
our dog sat in
Dad's chair
and brought
himself
his newspaper
and slippers.

Then he put
on the TV.
Like Dad,
he wouldn't
give up
the remote.

When bedtime
rolled around,
he read us
a story.
As usual,
we didn't
understand
a word.

Like Dad,
he gave us
a goodnight kiss.
Well, actually,
it was a
goodnight lick.

Boy, it was fun
having the dog
dress like Dad...

If only tomorrow
the cat dressed
like Mom.